M000317744

SOUL FORCE

SOUL**FORCE**
A Story about the
Rebirthing of Divine Presence
in a Postmodern World

Lloyd Griffith

Raleigh, North Carolina

© 2021 Lloyd Griffith
All rights reserved. Copying or use of this material without
express written consent by the author is prohibited by law.

"Here I Am, Lord" by Dan Schutte © 1981, 2003, OCP.
All rights reserved. Used with permission.

ISBN paperback: 978-1-945209-16-1
ISBN ebook: 978-1-945209-17-8
Library of Congress Control Number: 2021907945

Published by Clear Sight Books, Raleigh, North Carolina
Cover image by Laura Overman

Dedicated
in memory of Jerry Johnson,
who joined me in the telling of this story,
and
in gratitude to the many sojourners
in our centering prayer and contemplative
worship groups who supported the recovery of
the soul force in my own life.

Contents

Foreword

For many people today, there is no such thing as universal truth. Belief in an unconditional spiritual reality is beyond their range of comprehension. And yet this story is about the re-birthing of such a divine presence in our time. Our attentiveness to the spiritual domain awakens us to a divine truth, a soul force, in the concrete realities of life.

I am writing this story during a time when the world as we know it seems to be falling apart. Every day, some area of our world faces the catastrophe of extreme weather. Our daily sources of information are filled with hatred and discord, exacerbating the growing divide of us vs. them. The COVID-19 pandemic is returning in a new wave of infections and hospitalizations that promise more suffering and disorder. The future of the tenuous economy is increasingly bound to the fates of others around the globe, putting the financial future on a roller-coaster ride with no one controlling the speed.

In these times, for many of us our mental and emotional health is in danger. We reach into our inherited "backpacks" with their collection of acquired resources, beliefs, and stories that help us get what we want out of life, and we realize they are inadequate. Any sense of what we understood as truth, objectivity, science, or religion has been slowly abandoned. These things on which many of us depended for power and control are not holding. This postmodern world is skittering off into chaos. We grope for an answer to the question "Where is our authority now?" Without an answer to this fundamental question, we fall into disarray and ultimately chaos, as individuals and as a culture.

This story is about restoring the extraordinary experience of a divine center in the journey of an ordinary life. It's a journey of turning from our backpacks, our acquired myths of self-invention, to awaken to a deeper "I," a spiritual domain within each of us. This domain of life-force becomes our nourishment when we reach out with awe to the world around us. There, with our hearts open, we perceive a soul force, a spiritual energy of divine favor and goodwill that is present and active in us and in all of life.

Pilgrim can be a gentle companion on your journey to this intangible but very real dimension. Our passed-down backpacks have gotten heavy and cumbersome with the ways they filter our views of the world; they resist any attempts to set them aside. But this moment in time demands we take a fresh, unencumbered look at the relationship between us, the Divine, and the fragile world in which we live.

This new perspective can give us a portal to a whole new concept of divine truth. These times urge us to rethink everything we have been taught about human beings and the Holy. As we develop a new picture of each, it becomes clearer and clearer that the Divine is already in this place and we didn't even know it.

The Practice of
Letting Go

1

Coming to a Stop Sign

Questioning the Backpack

During the second semester of his doctoral program in chemical engineering at Georgia Tech, Pilgrim reached one of those crises in life that block the path we are following and cause us to change course. The degree was the final step in his carefully developed plan to pursue a career in research, following in the footsteps of his uncle.

Pilgrim had arrived at Georgia Tech after stellar progress as a dean's list student and starting guard on his undergraduate college basketball team. His stream of success came to an abrupt halt in a January conference with his faculty advisor, who expressed concerns about Pilgrim's readiness for doctoral-level research work and suggested he take some time off to strengthen those skills.

At this juncture Pilgrim recognized, probably for the first time, that his mental "backpack"—that collection of coping skills that he had acquired to get through life—was faulty. This backpack and its contents had been developing as long as he had, influenced by parents, teachers, coaches, and friends, all of whom had made an impact on him.

Its collection of tools for protection and survival began early when a patrol car pulled up to the front door of a two-bedroom, one-bath house nestled in a small, rural community twenty miles outside of Greenville, South Carolina. The quiet boundaries of the neighborhood were bordered by the Ingrams' rambling ranch house on one corner and the Teals' two-story brick house on the other. The officer's words dropped a bomb on that peaceful place. He reluctantly informed Pilgrim's mother, "Your husband has been arrested for driving under the influence."

His family's secret had been exposed, revealing the inconsistent and unpredictable world in which Pilgrim lived. Even before that ominous moment, Pilgrim had been filling his backpack with coping skills to survive in his unstable world. To protect himself, he pursued athletics—one of the few ways for a teenager in a small Southern town to win praise and approval.

Athletic accomplishments became an obsession. His backyard was converted into an arena framed by a one-car garage, a neighbor's fence, a row of thorny rose bushes, and a rusty set of swings. This imaginary coliseum became the stage for many tournaments in which Pilgrim, time after time, made the final shot to win the game.

Actual success on the high school basketball team became Pilgrim's way of earning approval and placating the increasing tension and disruption in his home. It diverted attention away from his family's secret and focused more on the positive things in his life.

Pilgrim developed a reputation as a "nice" guy. His classmates experienced him as trying to please and make them feel better. For his age, he was unusually good at listening and demonstrating empathy. After losses, he would anxiously apologize for letting others down: "I can't believe I missed that layup" or

"I'm sorry I didn't guard him closer" or "I hate that I dropped that pass."

This pattern of pleasing others became the default "app" in his increasingly cumbersome backpack. His automatic response to every circumstance was to be helpful with anything someone else needed. He would first focus on winning the other person's approval, diverting his attention away from himself. This response became his guide for surviving in an inconsistent and uncertain world and for getting what he needed to protect himself.

This adaptive backpack worked fine until Pilgrim came to the stop sign held up by his graduate school faculty advisor. His deficiency in research skills blocked the carefully planned path into the future. At this marker moment, being nicer did not help. Pleasing others did not help. The "backpack" he carried to survive and protect himself was not working here. He was lost and did not know what direction to go. In his years of automatically striving to please others, he had lost his own sense of self.

Glimmers

With graduate school off the table for the foreseeable future, Pilgrim found himself submerged in a constant flow of anxious thoughts as he tried to regain some control over his changing circumstances. He took a job teaching science at an all-boys boarding school with the hope of strengthening his research skills. However, the apathy of his students and the constant attention to supervision gradually drained away his energy for this new path. The routine of daily classroom preparations and the boredom of repetitive science experiments wilted his enthusiasm for biological research. The hopeful optimism that once flooded his thoughts shrank to a dribble. He did not know what he wanted to do.

Like all aspiring scientists, Pilgrim kept a lab notebook of sorts—a journal—and when he was writing, his attention changed. He was more attentive to his significant daily encounters than he was to the torrent of thoughts rushing through his mind. Quiet moments in the evenings when the students were in bed became a welcome retreat from the occupational treadmill driven by the "success apps" in his backpack.

During these peaceful moments he withdrew his racing mind from the plethora of events that filled his day and became more attentive to the moment. Inevitably there would be several days when he was consumed with controlling the circumstances in his life and would make no journal entry. But when there was time to catch up with his journaling, he temporarily let go of his "monkey mind" that jumped from one thing to another long enough to return to that peaceful inner silence.

His journal became a sanctuary. Over time the content of his journals expanded beyond edited "lab notes" to include details that attracted his attention throughout the day. Gradually this regular practice of journaling took him beyond the continuing flow of his thoughts to enter a dialogue with his own experiences.

One such significant encounter occurred in the school gym in the middle of junior varsity basketball practice. When he sat down in the bleachers to catch a glimpse of the afternoon practice, the musty smells and ricochet sounds brought back memories of his high school and college days. Unexpectedly, his attention was drawn to a huddle of players in a corner of the gym. He overheard one of the leaders encouraging his teammates, "Let's finish strong! Everyone pull together: with that spirit, we'll be our best."

That nudge to "spirit" struck a chord that ignited memories of Pilgrim's own experience of that elusive team spirit during his college days. Unlike the current draining experience of the classroom and lab, his memory of this other energy was life enhancing. When his college teams had found it, they were better. The possibility of rekindling the spirit he had known in athletics twinkled faintly in his consciousness.

Its glimmer persisted long enough to get recorded. That evening as he journaled about the events of the day, he remembered the motto he had noticed over in the corner where the team had gathered: "That they may value the Unseen and the Intangible—for of these Reality is fashioned." He edited his "research notes" with his own thoughts of somehow returning to athletics:

February 20. Overwhelmed by a deepening sense of doubt about myself, I was unexplainably drawn toward that huddle of young players in the corner of the gym. In a flash, out of nowhere,

coaching surfaced as a possibility.
Strange! I had never considered it as a
career. It did not have nearly the status
my uncle enjoyed as a research scientist.

Something More

Turning his thoughts away from anxiousness
about his future, Pilgrim noticed something
more. The glimmer of coaching benevolently
wedged its way into his quiet mind. Its twinkle
in his consciousness was a gift of something
more; it was not his, and certainly it was not
the team's. It was more like an under-glimmer
whose faintly luminous quality was barely
perceptible at first.

The brief flicker was an intangible, vague
desire toward something he missed rather
than an intentional use of his mental backpack to get something he wanted. The glow
of this desire was more intimate, emerging
from someplace deeper than his fabricated
backpack.

2

Awakening to a Spiritual Domain

Putting Down the Backpack

Pilgrim left the private school to become the assistant basketball coach and a science teacher at Washington Junior High School. He enjoyed the predictable routine of classes and the practices filled with close personal relationships with young, enthusiastic students. His family settled in, with June, his wife, staying at home with their two-year-old daughter, Sally, while Ben, their five-year-old son, started preschool at the Methodist church in their neighborhood. Almost unconsciously, Pilgrim quickened his pace in this new job, rushing to accomplish more and build on his success in the eyes of others.

As his accomplishments grew, he imagined moving on to coach his own team.

This daydream imploded when he was passed over for the school's head basketball coach position. A former assistant had applied to return and had been quickly hired. This unanticipated change was disheartening. The upward pathway Pilgrim had imagined evaporated. Facing this disappointment, Pilgrim was determined to work even harder to prove himself.

His enthusiasm was quickly depleted as he fell back into a comfortable rut of busily pleasing others. His complacency was breached a month later with an announcement in the school system newsletter of an opening for a basketball coach at Lincoln High School. Unlike the junior high school, which was larger and had several coaches for most sports, Lincoln was smaller and more urban and had only one coach for their basketball program.

In spite of this difference, Pilgrim went to visit the school and was immediately impressed with Don Knuckles, the principal at Lincoln. His faculty, two of whom Pilgrim had spoken with prior to the visit, had described

him as "aggressive, tough, and excessive."
Pilgrim saw that side of Don in the way he
directed the interview, but he also experienced him as an all-or-nothing kind of person
who was fully engaged in his work for the
school.

Don did not seem to be playing games when
he explained the school's mission to serve the
impoverished neighborhoods around the
school. This authentic sense of purpose was
a bright contrast to the normal educational
career path toward bigger schools with larger,
more impressive budgets.

As Pilgrim journaled that evening, this
sense of purpose beyond job security and
advancement was a strong attraction:

*January 22. I was so excited by my visit
to the school. It was different somehow. I was energized by the sense of
mission that seemed to fill the place.*

Attractive as this opportunity appeared,
the thought of moving into a less upscale
neighborhood across town curtailed Pilgrim's
initial enthusiasm. More immediate concerns
for his pregnant wife and two young children
pushed this fanciful idea aside. Comfort and
security for his family anchored him to his

current job and neighborhood. He allowed this attractive glimmer to drift past.

However, this wall of resistance was shattered a few weeks later in a bedroom conversation with June. Their relationship of twelve years had started with Pilgrim's attraction to her good looks and assertiveness. He grew to appreciate her affinity for life. While he assessed himself to be more like the principal at the high school, more calculating and controlling, she was open and responsive to life happening around her each moment. She never seemed to stop making improvements.

As they were getting ready for bed, Pilgrim shared his reservations about the new position at Lincoln High School. June was aware of Pilgrim's growing discontent in his current position. His vague malaise magnified her sadness at the loss of two friends who had recently moved out of town. Feeling ready for a change herself, she encouraged Pilgrim to take a closer look at this new opportunity.

Her openness to this possibility drew Pilgrim's attention away from himself and his fear of not pleasing his wife. Suddenly the position at the high school shone with a

new luster. As he journaled about their conversation just before turning out the lights,
Pilgrim literally felt the weight of his backpack slip off:

> **February 12.** *June's openness trig-
> gered my own. I surrendered the fear
> of disappointing her and suddenly felt
> like it was the first day of practice at the
> beginning of the season. I was full of
> energy and excited by this opportunity
> at Lincoln.*

Insight

Pilgrim was invited to return to the school for
a second interview for the varsity basketball
coach vacancy. Surprisingly, the meeting
with the principal and key members of the
faculty centered more on stories of students'
successes than on athletic accomplishments.
Clubs, service projects, and parental involvement were all part of the expanding energy
of the school. The administration's focus on
student aspirations and successes was more
important than standardized testing achieve-
ments or athletic accomplishments. Pilgrim's
deep yearning for this type of education found
its voice in his journal:

February 29. *I loved the tone in today's meeting. It focused on things that felt life-giving, which is so different from the draining concerns about victories and defeats that occupy most coaches. The invitation to join them resonated with something stirring deep within me.*

A couple of weeks later on a trip to the pharmacy for first-aid supplies, Pilgrim bumped into the Reverend Anna Finlayson. Anna had been his pastor for four years at Trinity Avenue Presbyterian Church. She was appreciated by her congregation as both a pastor and a prophet. Her preaching was well known for uncovering the hidden injunctions to be right, safe, respectable, organized, and in control that confine a life to what is known. But she was loved for the trust and acceptance she offered that encouraged people, whoever they were, to take responsibility for themselves instead of being seduced by or dependent on others.

Drawn by the comfort and strength of this relationship, Pilgrim shared with Anna his quandary about leaving his current familiar position for a venture into an uncertain future. Through these comments and from several earlier discussions with him, Anna recognized that Pilgrim had reached the end of his service at the junior high school.

She assured him, "You have done a good job at the school and developed skills that will be useful in many places."

Pilgrim resisted this gentle nudge. He quickly explained, "I am concerned about the safety of the new neighborhood and un-proven schools for my children."

Anna pointed out, "Pilgrim, I hear your hesitancy, but I also hear your excitement for this school and its mission. You don't have to give in to your reservations! Be grate-ful for this opportunity coming your way."

Back in his office this conversation lin-gered in Pilgrim's consciousness. Anna's comment "You don't have to give in to your reservations" clarified something resonating deep within Pilgrim. Through the torrent of anxious thoughts racing through his mind, a deep yearning for the position at Lincoln resurfaced. This insight just would not let him go.

He quickly jotted down his intuition on a piece of paper lying on his desk:

March 17. *Anna was right. Everything I've done so far has been preparation for this new position. If I don't take it, I'll lose the vision coming to life in me right now.*

A Life-Light

This insight was a light in Pilgrim's own life that was guiding him now. It was different from the ordinary flow of events that made up his day. It was deeper than his anxious attempts to control his future or Anna's efforts to be helpful. It was an intuitive truth emerging from his own life beyond the confines of his rational thinking. However blind he might have been to this deeper reality before, he had awakened to an unseen and intangible desire for this new position that would not let him go.

Pilgrim's insight about the vision coming into his life—this little light—was easy to miss and often went unnoticed. Its stirrings were no louder than the thumping of his heart. There were earlier times when he held the reins of control so tightly that these inner stirrings were obscured. But this time when, with June's encouragement, he released the reins of his attention long enough, he perceived a spiritual dimension of life. A life-light with glimmers and insights illumined his consciousness. His journal that same evening continued:

March 17 (continued). It was like a sip of cool spring water bubbling up within me. My enthusiasm for Lincoln seemed to be growing stronger and stronger. It was time to write a letter accepting their offer. Something powerful was at work in this decision. I just can't name it.

3

Departing for the Spiritual Domain

Letting Go of the Backpack

Pilgrim accepted the invitation to become head coach and faculty member at Lincoln High School. The announcement of this move put a cloud over the end-of-year celebrations at his old school. Students and faculty alike at Washington Junior High grieved the loss of Pilgrim's exuberance for teaching and personal support for struggling students.

As Pilgrim was beginning his final reports before leaving, Wallace Thompson, who had been Washington's principal for the last ten years, announced his retirement. While this decision had been anticipated for a couple of years, its timing on the heels of Pilgrim's unanticipated move was a surprise.

The chair and vice chair of the parents association made a plea for Pilgrim to re-consider leaving during this time of major transition. Their intervention pushed the "on" button to the pleasing "app" in his backpack. This app had been on sleep mode as Pilgrim prepared to follow the glimpse of life-light to Lincoln High, but this hint of disappoint-ing these parents raised old fears of losing control. Their request snared Pilgrim's atten-tion, tempting him to abandon his plans for leaving.

He was stretched between a deep yearn-ing for this new opportunity at Lincoln and his reluctance to disappoint the people at Washington. Some days he felt boldly confi-dent about striking out in a new direction, sure that he was responding to an authentic life-light. Other days he fretted about displeas-ing his colleagues, the students, and their parents for some risky pie-in-the-sky dream. His every step forward met resistance from the tyrannical "app" fueled by a fear of disap-pointing others. This tension pulling in his life filled the notes in the journal that evening:

May 17. *At first I was angry about the parents meddling in my plans. But guilt about leaving at such a bad time quickly pushed that anger aside. After talking so much about teamwork, this move to a new school at this time felt selfish. Maybe I should reconsider?*

The next afternoon Pastor Anna came by the school to check on Pilgrim's plans for moving. She had been supporting Pilgrim, as she did many others in the congregation, through this pivotal life change. With a pastoral ear open to Pilgrim's doubts and a prophetic eye on the life-light to which he was awakening, she had nurtured his blossoming attention to the spiritual domain by encouraging him to put some limits, boundaries, around his automatic response to help.

When Anna arrived, Pilgrim was busy shuffling more notes he had received from prominent members of the parents association. She intentionally interrupted this random business to invite Pilgrim on a short walk along the quiet creek that flowed through the woods behind the school.

Away from the bustling activity of a junior high school at the end of the day's classes,

Pilgrim confessed, "I'm wavering about leaving." He couldn't seem to get out of his racing mind, and he was reluctant to let go of control and trust anything more than the automatic response in his backpack. This accumulation of inherited beliefs and personal apps gave him some illusion of control and served as the authority with which he was most familiar.

Pastor Anna's response changed the direction of the conversation. "You can't please everyone. Let go of such an inflated sense of yourself and put a boundary around that automatic response that leads you in this dangerous direction. Your real work is now at Lincoln High. Go. The timing is right."

Her words shifted Pilgrim's attention from the tumultuous outpouring of anxious thoughts about not pleasing those at the junior high. In that freedom, Pilgrim was open to events and encounters in the moment. In the quiet he was free to experience the life-light in the here and now. When the pastor left, Pilgrim quickly jotted down his impression on a blank piece of paper on his desk:

May 18. A veil dropped from my eyes. I realized I was deceiving myself trying to

please everyone. Putting limits around
that fraud freed me from feeling indis-
pensable. Suddenly my eyes opened to
everything going on around me.

Aha Moment

Two days later, Pilgrim went to Lincoln High
School to begin his preparations for the move
there. The morning was filled with meetings
with the principal, the assistant principal for
student performance, the athletic director,
and the school nurse. Each conversation
was filled with excitement and lofty expectations about his joining the staff. When the
time came to leave, he was overwhelmed
with the magnitude of the responsibilities he
was assuming. A vintage sense of inadequacy
returned as he heard the flood of accolades
for the coach he was replacing. The growing
excitement for this move was doused by the
reality of high expectations surrounding it.
Suddenly, as his old school looked more
secure, predictable, and friendly, his wavering
about leaving returned.

These growing doubts heightened the
tension in his decision to purchase a new
house for the move. Prior to all the uproar

with Wallace's retirement and the pleas from the parents association, Pilgrim had put his house up for sale. Now the fear of having to carry two mortgages at the same time made the change more ominous. Almost daily he was tempted to withdraw his plans and stay put in his old school and home.

But June was attracted by the new house and all the possibilities that the new location offered. Her attention on the possibilities in the present moment nudged Pilgrim to resist his stream of thoughts about comfort and security and to keep his mind open to the moment.

The last opportunity to abandon his plans came as Pilgrim and June sat in a real estate agent's office ready to make an offer on a new home. Strengthened by June's openness to this opportunity, Pilgrim hesitantly moved forward with completing the sale contract.

Just before putting pen to paper, they were rescued by an unexpected telephone call. The agent handling the sale of their old home congratulated them on an acceptable purchase offer, protecting them from the precipice of overwhelming debt.

In this call some threshold was crossed. The message was like many in that office every week. But some extra increment of meaning had been added to Pilgrim's awareness. The call changed in appearance, revealing a life-light. A previously untapped spiritual force reached out to support this move. Pilgrim was connected to a vast reservoir of the spirit that was deeper than his intellect, emotion, or volition. His awakening to this spiritual domain in his life radiated through his journal that evening:

> *May 20. When I sat in that office making the down payment, I felt like I was dropping a noose over my own neck. That miraculous call cut the rope just in time. My old house sold!! My doubts lifted. I wasn't alone.*

Thin Places

This telephone call was a "thin place" where the life-light broke through the concrete realities of the moment. In that ordinary phone call, a deeper level of reality intersected with Pilgrim's daily circumstances. The boundary between the two levels of reality suddenly became soft, porous, and permeable. A curtain momentarily lifted, and Pilgrim perceived a spiritual force in his life.

Pilgrim awakened to a new life—a spiritual domain revealing a presence much larger than he had ever imagined. Putting boundaries around his automatic responses set him free to experience this ethereal domain close at hand. Its presence pushed aside his inherited picture of the Holy as "elsewhere." The thin veil between the physical and the spiritual briefly lifted, and Pilgrim awakened to an in-dwelling spirit revealed in the concrete realities of his own life.

This truth-bearing moment revealed the probability of a heaven close at hand. When Pilgrim paused to reflect on his life, he re-membered other times when his conscious-ness had been enlarged with insights that pulsated with life-giving energy. It was there in conversations in the classroom; it was there while he was on the field coaching; it was there with his family around the dinner table; it was there sitting together with June in the evening when life slowed down; and it was there when he was alone quietly writing in his journal. This indwelling spirit seemed far more accessible and personal than he had been taught it was. It was near enough to touch, feel, and catch a glimpse of for himself.

The Practice of
Holy Listening

4

Watching for the Soul Force

Paying Closer Attention

Pilgrim's attentiveness to this newly discovered spiritual domain was diverted early in his tenure at Lincoln High School. In the first week of classes after the summer break, he was enjoying lunch at the teachers' table with Bernie Copper, the assistant principal for student performance, and Holly Frank, the school nurse. Their cordial conversation was interrupted by Harry, a freshman, who slammed the cafeteria doors open and stormed over to an empty table in the back of the room.

None of Harry's classmates made any attempt to go over to the table. Their reluctance to get involved with an obviously angry student was echoed by the detachment of the other two staff members. Bernie excused himself to meet with the principal about re-arranging the seating plan in the auditorium, and Holly quickly moved to the next table to pass out lunchtime medications.

Pilgrim's automatic response to such un-expected interruptions, especially one filled with anger, was to avoid the conflict and, like his lunch table companions, let his busy after-noon schedule distract him from the crisis. But this time he intentionally went against his first inclination.

He took his lunch to the table at the back of the cafeteria and joined the angry student. The sinister silence at the secluded table was conspicuous. Harry's head was buried in his folded arms. His body language reinforced the wall he'd raised around himself.

Pilgrim took the ham and cheese sand-wich from his bag and offered half to the still-furious freshman. His advance was met by the same stoic demeanor. However, a home-made chocolate chip cookie reserved for des-sert proved to be a door opener. Its inviting aroma and extra chocolate chips could not be resisted. The student accepted the cookie and promptly devoured it. Through this small opening Pilgrim slipped an invitation to visit his office, where more cookies had been stashed for an afternoon snack.

The change in Pilgrim's response had been intentional. Since his early recognition of the spiritual domain, Pilgrim had questioned whether it was possible to be more deliberate in welcoming the life-light into his life rather than randomly falling into it at various times.

His answer had come during a coaching clinic he'd attended that summer. Coach Tony Shelton was the clinic's leader and one of the most successful college coaches in the state. He introduced team spirit as more a heart thing than a head thing. "Its presence is not something concrete onto which you can grab. It is more an ethereal flow in the relationships that make up the team. But its presence is powerful."

Pilgrim made a quick connection between this introduction of team spirit and the elusive energy of the life-light he had experienced in deciding to change jobs. His attention was hooked as the coach took them further.

"Team spirit," he cautioned, "is not something a coach can control. You can only nurture its growth by encouraging players to connect to the team more than to themselves. This requires listening differently, in a nonjudgmental way that seeks to understand the other's point of view.

"While this change in response sounds simple, doing it in the heat of an athletic contest is challenging. Most young people have some illusion that they can find a way to be in control like the adults in their life. The regular practice of listening nonjudgmentally breaks through this inflated self-centeredness, opens their minds, and enables them to appreciate others' contributions to the team's success.

"This kind of listening changes the relationship from a power struggle to a partnership that creates a larger, more powerful team presence. The individual players discover a whole new domain of experience that is bigger than any individual. The outcome of this deeper connection to others instead of self is magical."

Coach Shelton concluded his comments with a story that was familiar to many in the room. In the third quarter of a close game in the conference tournament, neither team had been able to establish a convincing lead. At the start of the fourth quarter one coach changed from a one-on-one defense to zone defense based on a suggestion from one of his guards. That simple change, which emerged from an act of nonjudgmental listening during a time-out, proved to be the difference that led to victory.

During the remainder of the clinic, the coaches practiced Coach Shelton's motto: "Listening is more an active than passive response to the challenges you face." In pairs, they practiced role-plays by clearing their minds of distractions and listening nonjudgmentally for their partner's point of view. As the clinic concluded, Pilgrim realized he had his answer. Listening this way made him more attentive to events in the moment and opened his mind to glimmers from a spiritual domain.

Brilliance

Pilgrim was intent on paying closer attention to Harry when he invited the angry student to his office for more cookies. At first Harry went to the window and refused to sit in the chair beside the desk. With his arms held tightly against his chest and his eyes riveted to the floor, Harry had no intention of talking. When Pilgrim brought out the bag with the few remaining cookies, the student reached over and knocked them on the floor.

Pilgrim withheld his first inclination to grab the ungrateful boy by the arm and shake the disrespect out of him. Instead, he calmly picked up the bag of cookies and took his seat facing the student and the empty chair.

"I'm in no hurry. I've got time for you, and I want to know what made you so mad."

After ten torturous minutes of silence Harry furiously shouted, "Three big guys caught me on the stairwell, grabbed my arms, and told me to give them money for lunch."

Pilgrim, resisting a pat response to bullying, focused his full attention on the young man and asked him, "What did you do?"

Harry shot back, "Gave it to them!"

Pilgrim, again quietly and trustingly, hoping to see the experience from the student's eyes, questioned, "Did that help?"

The freshman was quick to respond. "I thought the guys might like me if I gave them the money."

Pilgrim, pondering the impact of this rejection, continued listening for something more. "Something made you really mad just before you came in the cafeteria."

Harry, obviously hurt, responded, "They just ran off with my money."

Pilgrim pulled his chair a little closer to the student and reached out to touch the arm of the chair as he clarified what he'd heard. "It sounds like you got shoved aside?"

The young student, more ashamed than anything, said in almost a whisper, "Yes. Those guys have been pushing me around and running off since school started."

Pilgrim, following along, asked, "Is there anywhere else you're being pushed around?"

Harry was quiet for a long time. He appeared more at ease in the chair he had finally taken when he said, "Only sometimes at home when my dad gets mad. Like last week he took my dog away. He shouted, 'Harry, you are less than worthless! You can't even remember to put out the garbage.'"

Pilgrim, drawing a little closer to test out what he sensed, responded, "That sounds like it hurt even more than today's put-down."

Harry, getting more secure in this sheltered, accepting atmosphere, added, "That wasn't the first time Dad took away my things when he was angry. He did the same thing with a pair of skis and a BB gun before that."

Pilgrim, moving slowly, asked, "What did you do about your dad giving away your things?"

The young man responded with a look of desperation as he raised his head to face Pilgrim, "Nothing! What am I supposed to do? He's bigger than me and sometimes gets really mad . . . especially when he drinks." There was a long pause in the conversation. "I worry a lot."

At that moment, the comment "I worry a lot" stood out with brilliance unlike the rest of the conversation. Its intensity caught Pilgrim's attention. The bullying, the anger, the rejection, and dysfunction at home generated a clear cry for help to redirect his attitude and behaviors to value himself despite his father's misbehavior.

Pilgrim, responding to this glimmer, reached out. "How about helping me sort through some old uniforms and equipment to get ready for preseason basketball practice? It starts next week."

With a smile pushing aside the hurt in his eyes, the young student enthusiastically asked, "Can I come this afternoon?"

As Pilgrim journaled that evening, he was conscious of the "thin" place in this conversation where the spiritual energy had broken through. His intentional connection to this angry student, listening to him instead of to his own defensive thoughts, opened his mind to deeper vitality in the moment. He wrote:

September 5. *Suddenly my awareness shifted in the conversation. Harry's cry for help screamed like the blare of a megaphone. Paying closer attention, I couldn't miss it.*

Illumination

Harry's cry for help was a revelation of life-light. Its illumination in Pilgrim's consciousness was not so much a thing he observed as it was an inner resonance whose intensity was more pronounced than other segments of the conversation. Its brightness emerged in reverberations between the student's pain and Pilgrim's intentional close attention to the moment.

As with the team spirit on which he had been coached, when Pilgrim reached out to Harry when others had passed him by, he went beyond his acquired backpack to open his mind to the dynamics of life flowing around him.

5

Waiting for the Soul Force

Becoming Intimate with the Moment

Pilgrim's challenge was staying open to the spiritual flow he had begun to glimpse in the circumstances of his life. And Frankie was just such a summons.

Frankie had been a troublemaker all through junior high school. Whenever a teacher drew the line on classroom discipline, Frankie would be the first to cross it. It was an automatic response for which all the teachers had learned to brace themselves.

One day in Pilgrim's PE class, Frankie was continually pushing whoever happened to be next to him. His shoves were not subtle; they were forceful enough to catch everyone's attention. In the past Pilgrim would have responded quickly and firmly, sending Frankie to the principal's office and reasserting his control. But on this day, he took a different tack: he invited Frankie to take a break from the other students and have a seat on the sidelines.

Pilgrim was just back from participating in a fall weekend YMCA family camp that had expanded his skills in listening. From Friday to Sunday, he and his family had gathered with thirty-six other families at a remote campsite fifteen miles out of town. Forty-two cabins and a rustic dining hall ringed a twenty-acre freshwater reservoir that invited fishing, kayaking, and swimming. Three trails meandered in a dense forest, guiding hikers through beautiful wildflowers, past small animals, and into deep quiet. The weekend was a welcome break for fun and for strengthening relationships in his family.

Several hour-long workshops were part of the program. A variety of interesting topics were offered, including discipline techniques, communication, school readiness, and child development. Pilgrim's attention was immediately drawn to a workshop on conflict resolution. The workshop leader was the mother of a student to whom Pilgrim had devoted a lot of time, helping him recover from a dislocated shoulder. With a master's degree in child development and nine years of experience at Project Soar, a school-system-wide resource for training parents to help children succeed at home as well as at school, Rose was especially well qualified to lead this workshop.

The workshop focused on successful conflict resolution. During the first part of the hour, Rose pointed out how circumstances could trigger a power response that intensified the conflict because one or more parties were trying to control the outcome. She then introduced a language of acceptance that changed the environment and thus the potential outcome of the conversation. The key in this change was to resist the automatic inclination to manipulate the outcome and instead withhold judgment and connect to the situation in a compassionate, more open way.

As the group practiced working with different conflictual situations, participants began to recognize how tethered they were to a language of control and the intentional effort they had to make to resist this pull and openly accept the other person as they themselves would want to be accepted. Rose brought out the importance of this change in behavior with examples of such acceptance that moved the parties in conflict beyond their win-lose approach to wait for a solution that worked for everyone.

Rose's concluding words stayed with Pilgrim long after the workshop ended: "Love like this connects you to a flow of deeper meanings that move beyond the power struggle."

Inspiration

When Pilgrim sat down with Frankie that morning, he was intent on listening more compassionately. It didn't take Frankie long to unload.

"You are just like all the other teachers who have it in for us. All you want to do is shove us around and make us shut up."

Pilgrim did not take the bait being thrown to him. Withholding his immediate negative reaction, he quietly held Frankie with trust in his words as he responded, "You act mad at everyone—teachers too. What's making you so angry?"

Frankie was quick and emphatic with his answer. "You are just like my dad, who pushes me and my brothers around at home."

In this outburst, Pilgrim heard the pain Frankie was feeling at home behind the anger spilling out in the conflicts at school.

Pilgrim's attention leaped back to a conversation earlier that morning, well before the PE class assembled. Frankie had been the topic of conversation among several teachers who anticipated encounters with him during the day. The AD declared that Frankie should be sent to the guidance counselor as the quickest, least disruptive response to his misbehavior.

Reluctant to disappoint his supervisor, Pilgrim was tempted to follow the AD's guidance—to give up on waiting and take some firm action. But rather than rushing in with prescribed answers to this cry for help, Pilgrim went slowly, resisting his inclination to send Frankie to the office. He continued to try to understand Frankie's point of view. "It must seem like no one cares," he said.

Frankie, after a long pause, said, "I guess. All I get is crap from everybody."

Just at that moment, with Pilgrim struggling

to keep his attention open, a nagging concern about sweaty jerseys dropped on the locker room floor at the end of practice popped into his mind again. The need to collect those dirty shirts and get them in the laundry had been bugging him all day. Suddenly, in the midst of this conversation with Frankie, an answer emerged. Frankie's need for acceptance and Pilgrim's need to manage the uniforms connected in an aha moment: Frankie could be the team manager.

This inspiration was an animating energy springing from the conversation. Frankie's action brought the moment to Pilgrim's attention, but the meaning that was conveyed depended on Pilgrim's waiting for it. Its life-giving influence was not something Pilgrim could control. But in listening compassionately to this troubled student, Pilgrim held his heart open to the life-light present in the moment. He allowed the experience itself to speak to him.

A Still Small Voice

This animating influence Pilgrim received was a whisper of a still small inner voice. It was a different kind of presence from the concrete materiality with which he was most familiar. This energy was invisible like the wind; Pilgrim couldn't tell where it came from, but it was clearly discernable. Pilgrim perceived it, and its vibrations stirred him to action.

"Could you help me with these uniforms?" Pilgrim asked.

Without a moment's hesitation Frankie reached for a jersey that had been left on the back of a chair. With a smile replacing the anger shrouding his face, he asked, "Where does this go?"

Pilgrim's recognition of a small voice that only he had heard was evident in his journal reflections later that evening:

October 21. The spark to make Frankie a manager was perfect. It sure wasn't Frankie's plan, or mine, when our chat started. But when the inspiration came, it was what we both needed at the time.

6

Knowing the Soul Force

Committing to Holy Listening

As one season at Lincoln High led into the next and the next, Pilgrim's enthusiasm for teaching and coaching waned with the increasing demands of those who wanted his help. Along with this unrelenting expansion of the responsibilities at school, June had started a long, costly chemotherapy protocol for breast cancer, and his aging parents had just moved into a retirement center four blocks from his home.

Late one afternoon in early April, Pilgrim ran into Principal Knuckles at the pharmacy where they had both stopped to pick up prescriptions. In their cordial conversation as they stood in line for service, Pilgrim learned that the current athletic director at the high school had just resigned to care for his father who had early signs of dementia.

Don Knuckles was straightforward on most things. He was regarded as one of the best principals in the system, recognized for getting things done swiftly and efficiently. He wasted no time offering his opinion that this opening was the best next step on Pilgrim's career path.

This unanticipated opportunity was one of those crossroads in life where the way forward was unclear. Pilgrim felt needed and appreciated in his current role as coach and teacher. The students and faculty welcomed his sensitivity and tireless efforts to be helpful. While his involvement in so many activities increased the stress in his life, it also gave him a sense of being indispensable.

On the other hand, the AD position that his principal had invited him to consider would lead him away from this invigorating contact with students and into more administrative responsibilities. But the new position did promise less investment in so many demanding personal relationships, especially the challenging ones that so often seemed to come his way, and it would increase the financial resources for his family's rising medical and retirement expenses.

When Pilgrim shared this conversation with June that evening following supper, his reservations about the attractive path up the educational ladder were clear. He anxiously explained as he sat down next to her, "I'm afraid of getting lost on that familiar track in the school system. It is so easy to become one more assistant in the gaggle and find yourself distracted by trying to grab little bits of power that might get you ahead of the others. I think I am going to tell him no thanks."

June's answer pushed against this automatic response. "You would be smart to find out more about the new role before you hastily turn it down," she said. June often nudged Pilgrim out of his backpack with its unconscious default reactions and invited him to be more attentive to the opportunities in the here and now.

Freed from his knee-jerk response, Pilgrim met with the principal the next day to find out more about the AD opening. He learned that for efficiency the old AD role had been expanded to include all the physical education programs at the adjacent junior high school. This change created a critical need for an experienced educator who was qualified to manage the program at both schools. In addition, the position was open immediately due to the quick departure of the previous AD.

Soul Force

Rather than rushing ahead to seize this attractive opportunity, Pilgrim waited, listening attentively for a life-light glimmering in this situation. His patience paid off when he was struck by a random comment as he and his basketball buddies walked off the court the next day. Following their regular lunchtime game, Bob, his best friend in the group, boasted, "Don't forget it's my turn to pay for lunch. Let's meet at Wendy's."

In the locker room, Pilgrim's deliberations about this new opportunity became the subject of their conversation. Pilgrim made clear his uneasiness with the potential imprisonment he feared in a large educational organization.

He anxiously explained, "I've seen school systems strangle people in red tape and suck all their energy away. In spite of the stress I'm dealing with right now, I would be crazy to give up the coaching and teaching I love."

Bob, a regional sales representative for a new line of jeans, observed, "It's not the titles in the organization that carry the real power. Power is tied to the money and who controls it. Just like lunch today—since I'm paying, I get to choose where we will go."

Bingo! A life-giving energy resonated in Pilgrim. Something deeper than the principal's offer and a concern over the hierarchy of a large organizational system sounded within. The significance of budget control intuitively surfaced in Pilgrim's consciousness. This insight revealed a way forward in the educational system. His consciousness of this deeper voice, this animating energy, appeared in his journal entry that evening.

April 19. Suddenly the clouds surrounding me seemed to part at Bob's comment. I perceived something more. Control of the budget was the life-giving step forward at this crossroads. It is an alternative that can be win-win.

His confidence in this inner voice was tested two days later when Principal Knuckles stopped by the gym for an answer. After a cordial review of the expanded responsibilities, the deliberations reached a perilous precipice. Don Knuckles explained that all the departmental budgets in the school were managed by the vice principal for finance.

Pilgrim courageously held on to his inspiration despite the possibility of disappointing the principal and presumptuously gambling away this opportunity. He proposed reorganizing the athletic department budget under this new AD position to facilitate the administration of new programs at the two schools.

Don's response astonished him. The performance-oriented principal, who rarely changed, agreed to modify the job description because he wanted this highly qualified candidate. He shifted accountability for the athletic budget to the AD.

In that modification, something clicked. Pilgrim experienced the soul force for himself. He became conscious of a life-giving energy flowing through this conversation. He perceived a Divine vitality present and active in the moment inviting him to step out onto a new path.

Heaven-Born

This incredible turn of events changed everything. The still small voice Pilgrim had experienced in the locker room conversation was something more than coincidence. It was the direct communication of life-giving energy from the core of his being. It surpassed the conjectures of a separate and distant Divine that he had inherited from his childhood. He heard, saw, and even tasted the care and love of this transcendent force in his own life.

At that moment, the Divine no longer lived "out there" in some faraway place. It had moved in with him, empowering him in a new direction. Pilgrim had recovered the integrity of his inner depth. The Divine spirit was bearing witness with his spirit in the concrete realities of life. The soul force was "in the boat with him." They were traveling together.

Pilgrim was a new person. He was heaven-born with an alternative consciousness of a soul force that existed beyond the inherited knowledge and packaged solutions of his backpack.

Realigned with a new authority, Pilgrim learned to see differently. His attention shifted from trying to control outcomes in the external world to heeding this life-giving energy of the soul force. This mystical experience of life-giving energy became his teacher as he practiced listening for it.

The Practice of
Following

7

Living in a New Country

Embracing the Soul Force

Pilgrim's new office at Lincoln High School was conveniently located near the main entrance to the gym, with a window that opened to a view of the three basketball courts below. On the adjoining wall was another, larger window that looked out on four athletic fields connecting the high school with the junior high.

When Pilgrim arrived on his first day, the bookcases and file cabinets were half full of programs inherited from previous ADs. It took most of the morning to squeeze his books and folders into the crowded space.

The accomplishments of the two previous

ADs were legendary. Both had been asser-
tive leaders who kept their hands on every
detail of the physical education program at
the high school. Pilgrim moved into the AD
office with an abundance of enthusiasm,
eager to follow in their successful footsteps.
But with the addition of the junior high
school the terrain had doubled in size.
Streaking like a thoroughbred with blinders
on, Pilgrim raced along the well-worn track
of management expectations carved out by
his predecessors. Focused on proving himself,
he was quickly consumed by the race to cover
two schools.

For the first six months of the school year
Pilgrim made frequent circuits between the
junior and senior high schools, feverishly
trying to stay involved in programs at both
places. The race halted abruptly when he
fainted at the wheel of his minivan on the
road between the schools. He crossed a lane
of oncoming traffic and rammed head-on
into a large oak tree. When he regained consciousness three days later, he squinted
through bandages into a room in the intensive care unit at the local hospital. With
multiple broken bones and his life maintained

by a ventilator, he was prematurely close to death.

At this stop sign on his life journey, Pilgrim automatically reached for the quickest way to heal his broken body. Why had he fainted? He sought answers in more specialists, more tests, and many different therapies. An extensive period of recuperation and many inconclusive tests drained away all illusions of controlling his recovery. The wreck brought a creeping awareness of his indisputable vulnerability and helplessness. He slipped into a dark night with an uncertain dawn.

Pilgrim struggled with the melancholy and uncertainty taking hold in his life. He could not turn off the torrent of things he should be doing racing through his mind. The default "app" raised his anxiety to not disappoint the administration at school. The pressure of these expectations was so intense that every time June visited he pleaded with her to bring his briefcase to the ICU. "I can't get behind on my to-do list!"

June, in her typical way, was more direct and in tune with the matters of the moment. During her brief visits she kept encouraging him to let go of all he had to do for the school and focus on getting well. Given their long relationship, she could confront his strong defenses long enough to catch his attention. "Pilgrim," she gently reminded him, "you can let the list go." And then on the next visit, somewhere during the conversation she unobtrusively slipped in, "You can stop worrying about disappointing others right now."

As Pilgrim's illusion of control continued to be eroded by the drips and monitors attached to his body, her words finally connected like a key that released the lock on his attention. He let go of the checklist and with it the compulsion to please those in authority at the school. In a flash, those binding expectations evaporated and his mind opened to everything going on in his hospital room. Before June left, he asked her to make an entry for him in his journal that she had brought from home:

February 28. Today I closed my briefcase and put it out of sight in the closet. I let go of any hope of finishing my to-do list. I realized I was crazy to worry about catching up. I stepped out of this incarceration and stepped into the much more immediate task of getting well.

Freed from the self-protective apps in his backpack, Pilgrim was able to watch for stirrings of the soul force in all life around him. Its glimmers reached him when he got out of the ICU. Beau Richards, the assistant AD, was one of his first visitors. Beau had been the AD at the junior high school before the position was merged with the senior high position. Beau's record as one of the few two-sport lettermen at the state university made him highly popular with students and parents. Beau's transition to this new role as assistant AD had been made easier by a significant increase in his salary and Pilgrim's seniority.

The relationship between the two following the staff reorganization had been professional. Pilgrim tended to look over Beau's shoulder, as he did with others, to ensure programs followed their carefully designed plans. But this visit to the ICU came following Pilgrim's decision to put his briefcase away in the closet, which left him more mindful of the moment.

Beau gave a full update on the programs at school. Due to his usual chattiness Pilgrim noticed how many of his own responsibilities

Beau had assumed during this confinement
in the hospital. When Beau finally paused to
catch a breath, Pilgrim's typically cautious
mind perceived in Beau a natural eagerness
to manage the problematic to-do list. When he
had Beau pull the two-page, single-spaced
list from his briefcase in the closet, his assistant was enthusiastic about this new level of
confidence Pilgrim was placing in him. A sigh
of relief could be heard in this life-light break-
ing through this thin place in the conversation.
That evening Pilgrim noted:

> *February 29. Aha! Beau really was
> different somehow. He had gotten so
> much done. I had a hunch he could
> handle the list fine! And he was ready
> when I put it in his hand. Funny—he
> was just what I needed at that moment.*

Several days later, a visit from Don
Knuckles challenged Pilgrim's fresh openness to life. Don, as Pilgrim had known since
his very first interview with the man, was a
practical, efficient commander who took few
prisoners in accomplishing his agenda. His
initial warm inquiries about recuperation
caught Pilgrim off guard. Pilgrim responded
forthrightly about discomfort with broken

bones and uncertainty about the length of his hospital stay. Don, his tone slightly more authoritative, yet still friendly, suggested the possibility of reassigning Pilgrim to be vice principal of student services.

This potential change activated the defensive "apps" in Pilgrim's backpack. Without thinking, Pilgrim grabbed the thread of his current AD position for protection. "My new role is just beginning to mesh at both schools," he protested. "It has taken this long just to get to know the faculty, students, and parents."

But Pilgrim caught himself from rushing further ahead defensively. His patience had been nurtured by visits from the hospital chaplain.

Paul Felder was the eldest of three ministers on the hospital staff. His first career as an army chaplain had taken him on two tours to Thailand and Cambodia. His exposure to Eastern spiritual traditions had awakened him to the availability of a spiritual path for individuals living ordinary lives, not one reserved for those following religious vocations.

When Pilgrim was moved out of the intensive care unit, Paul became a daily visitor.

The two connected over their stories as "perceived" star athletes in high school. Each visit began with favorite reminiscences of their athletic accomplishments. But the conversations would always return to Pilgrim's concern with controlling the outcome of his situation.

The chaplain, quietly and unassumingly, witnessed to the need to wait for the holiness present in all life, or its healing would never be known. As they visited day after day, Paul delicately joined Pilgrim on his journey through the dark night. His support, rather than giving answers, nurtured a compassion that was attentive to Pilgrim's life experiences.

Sometimes Paul gently prodded, "Do you have to please all the principals on the administrative staff?" And Pilgrim would slow down and reflect for a moment on the pressures overloading his life. Or they would be talking about the school's position on some issue like extra meals for disadvantaged children and Paul would ask Pilgrim, "What are your thoughts and concerns?" And Pilgrim would reflect for a moment on his own wants and needs instead of what he thought would please his principal, and he would gain a glimpse of clarity about himself.

Slowly, gradually, in these conversations Pilgrim began to be more attentive to himself and what he actually wanted rather than taking on what others wanted. As he began to respect himself as much as he did others, he awakened to the deeper meanings and alternate possibilities he had first become conscious of in the conflict management workshop with Rose.

This patience was present when he put aside his defensiveness to listen compassionately to Don's plan for the new vice principal. Don began with a compelling concern for a community of Iranian immigrants that had settled in an urban housing development two blocks from the high school. The language barrier made engaging the parents and involving their children in school almost impossible.

"Pilgrim," he said, "you have the skills and additional professional training to navigate these barriers and establish ways to serve this population."

These words breached the padlock Pilgrim had placed on his attention. Don's description of this vulnerable community awakened Pilgrim to their difficulty in acclimating to this new culture. Gradually their need took on a brightness in the conversation that somehow felt irresistible.

The vocal wrestling match between the principal and the coach continued long past the recommended hour for visitation. The tussle gradually pruned away the dross in the conversation. Finally, almost as a diversion, Pilgrim acknowledged the outstanding job Beau had done while he had been in the hospital.

Don, in a moment of inspiration, blurted out, "What if we promote Beau to associate AD and give him more responsibilities for the PE programs and free you up to work with the Iranian families while still continuing as AD?"

This inspiration resonated with life-giving energy. It came through a quiet inner voice from some mysterious source beyond Don's pushing and Pilgrim's resisting. Its invisible but clearly present energy resounded from deeper in Pilgrim's heart. Its illumination revealed the soul force emerging in Pilgrim's life.

March 7. *As we haggled over the job description, I experienced another voice. Its presence was life-giving. The change in Beau's job description went beyond the confines of this mundane conversation and touched on the miraculous.*

Pilgrim seized this inspiration to help the immigrant community, working it into his life. He signed up for a six-week course at the community college that was designed to help volunteers understand and support the social, emotional, and linguistic needs of immigrants. Students were guided to appreciate the diversity of backgrounds, situations, and needs of immigrants. As their awareness of the immigrants' needs increased, they learned to avoid projecting their personal values onto them.

The weekly class meetings incorporated workshops to strengthen listening skills in different contexts where volunteers might engage with immigrants. The challenge of ordering a meal in a local café with a Russian guest was eye-opening. The simple process of defining choices for lunch took fifteen frustrating minutes of working through a tri-fold menu. From the confusion of translating

wishes into another language, Pilgrim realized the primary desire of an immigrant,
just like his own desire, was to be seen as an
individual. As his respect grew, Pilgrim came
to see immigrants as people first.

Pilgrim reached out to Arman, the one
Iranian student who had made his way to
the high school. This young man's uncle had
immigrated to the United States ten years
earlier, and he had insisted his nephew at-
tend school to learn English. When Pilgrim
arranged a visit to the student's home, he
was welcomed into a modest, immaculately
clean, one-bedroom apartment. When Arman
got up to get some water, Pilgrim noticed the
refrigerator was nearly empty. Assuming their
resources were limited, Pilgrim inquired,
"Where do you like to shop? Can you find
what you need there?"

The mother, who spoke little English,
expressed her distress over the change in
her family's diet in this new country. With
Arman helping to translate, she complained
that her children now wanted to eat nothing
but pizza.

When Pilgrim shared some of his enlight-
ening adventures into this community with

his associate AD, Beau quickly responded with his frustrations in understanding this group. His Rotary Club had raised money to purchase sixteen bicycles for the children in the Iranian community.

"After three weeks," he explained, "those bikes were wrecks, lying around the neighborhood and never getting repaired."

The next time Pilgrim visited the family he noticed the accuracy of Beau's observation. When he asked Arman's mother about the broken bike on her front porch, she was almost ashamed to admit, "I am frightened by Arman's freedom to leave the neighborhood whenever he wants."

Gradually Pilgrim grew to recognize the Iranian people as individuals rather than as stereotypes. As he got to know them better, he perceived the same life-giving energy flowing through each of them that he had discovered in his own life. He realized that there were no quick fixes for the principal's desire to get these students better acclimated to the high school. The connection was more complicated. Integration would take patience and listening to build a connection, just like every other good relationship in the school.

Blessing

This complex answer was not the direction Pilgrim's principal had anticipated traveling. Don Knuckles operated with a one-size-fits-all educational philosophy and was looking for a quicker, simpler answer for this attendance problem. When he heard Pilgrim's assessment, he emphatically stated that funding for this outreach program would not be renewed at the end of the school year. He pointed to reductions in the revised operating budget that left him no choice.

Pilgrim agonized over this obstacle. Initially he was inclined to give in to Don's decision and abandon hopes for this immigrant family and its struggling community. He was tempted to stay in his principal's good graces by accepting this ultimatum and acquiescing to Don's decision.

But Pilgrim had grown particularly close to Arman's family and had witnessed their growing trust in the school. To end the program now would sever the vital ties the families were beginning to form with longtime residents and slow their progress toward full participation in the community.

A conspicuous comment from Pastor

Anna in her Sunday reflections encouraged Pilgrim to hold on to this life-light despite the obstacles and opposition. Her text was Matthew 4:1–11. She told the story of Jesus's journey into the desert following his baptism. There he was tempted by security, fame, and control of events and others. He resisted these enticements and entrusted his life to the Divine presence of which he was becoming conscious.

The timing of this sermon was serendipitous. Pilgrim left the service with a firmer grip on his consciousness of the soul force that had led him to this family. Rather than giving in to his principal's plan, Pilgrim continued looking for a way around this obstacle in his path.

His ally turned out to be Betty Hiner, who had taught with him at the junior high when their careers were just starting. They shared a common appreciation for the uniqueness of each child and became close colleagues as they designed special learning projects for their students. Betty had advanced to become director of student services for the school system. In this position she identified and implemented strategies for increasing

student use of services and student involvement in available programs. She also over-
saw the administration of the budget for
extracurricular activities, student services,
and events.

Pilgrim reconnected with her at a reception
for a new assistant superintendent. As they
renewed their friendship, Pilgrim brought
up his excitement for the outreach program
in which he was involved and its uncertain
future. Betty was interested in learning more.

A meeting with Betty, given her administrative position in the school system's hierarchy, was politically dangerous for Pilgrim.
He went to her office at the end of classes the
next day unsure of what the outcome might
be. Pilgrim shared his growing attachment to
Arman's family and the Iranian community to
which they had introduced him. He anxiously
added a concern about his principal's intention to eliminate this outreach program at the
end of the school year.

"I don't know where to go," he said. "I just
know this is not a quick fix—and it does need
fixing!"

Betty was moved by the depth of relationship Pilgrim had established with Arman's

family and the impact that relationship had had on changing his perception of these individuals who happened to be immigrants. She agreed to take his concern about this endangered program to the superintendent, Dr. Rodrigues Moreno.

A week later Pilgrim waited anxiously for a call from his principal about skirting the chain of command. Instead, he was surprised to hear from Betty, who said, "I presented your outreach program and its longer-term objectives to the superintendent's administrative committee. They were excited by these initial steps toward inclusion, and they wanted to support it as a systemwide project. They reached into the superintendent's special needs allocations to fund this outreach program at all high schools next year." She added, in her congratulations, that Dr. Moreno's experience as a Mexican immigrant had been helpful.

Words of gratitude filled Pilgrim's journal that evening:

> *May 10. A huge weight has been taken off my shoulders. All I can say is thank you for Betty. I have been given what I need at the moment. I was relieved . . .*

fortunate . . . blessed! Surely I have been
embraced by some divine favor or good-
will, not my own.

A New Country

Pilgrim was making his way in a new country,
a spiritual domain. His awareness of the
soul force upholding and empowering him
in the concrete circumstances of his life
gave him a more authentic sense of self. The
entire "do-it-yourself" universe that Pilgrim
had carried in his backpack for so long had
shattered and reassembled into a wholeness
more beautiful than he had thought possible.
The soul force, the presence of a Divine
spirit, was in this place and until now he
had not even known it. Its life-giving energy
reached out to him with the warm embrace
of an old friend.

This life-giving energy was present in
every moment. Like the gentle, firm nudge
of a shepherd's crook, it gave him what he
needed and guided him in the direction he
needed to go. Its presence connected Pilgrim
to a greater story, and even though he could
catch only a glimpse of it at any moment, he
sensed that this story was unending. He knew

this energy as an indwelling spirit, a "oneness" in his life where the soul force was traveling with him.

Pilgrim's fainting at the wheel of his car had been caused by vasovagal syncope, a fall in blood pressure triggered by a slowing of the heart. But his path out of the darkness was a gift of an indwelling soul force that would not let him go. His journal that evening revealed the restoration of well-being to his life:

> **May 25.** *I feel like a new person. My body is a lot better; I am well on the way to a full recovery. But there is something more, much more. I am different. I am not alone! I have glimpsed some essential ingredient that is in this boat with me.*

He knew! He knew for himself the soul force that would not let him go.

Afterword

Many of us have never experienced anything like this soul force. Most of us discount such reality or live off someone else's experience of this life-giving energy. We complacently get by on good behavior with no anticipation of, or vigilance for, a mysterious, incredible spiritual domain in our lives.

Pilgrim's story invites us to turn to, and become attentive to, the soul force reaching out in life. His journey reveals step-by-step practices of response that awaken us to this creative, life-giving energy that is present in all living things.

1. The journey begins with the practice of letting go of our backpacks. The choice to let go of doing and speaking all the time, to calm our minds, moves us away from the automatic responses carried in our inherited backpacks. In the stillness and freedom, we notice glimmers and insights from another domain of spiritual energy deep within.

2. The practice of holy listening connects us to this other domain. Instead of bemoaning the past or trying to control the future, we connect to life in the moment by listening to the other's point of view. We wait for the soul force by listening with compassion, instead of manipulation, loving others as we love ourselves. Holy listening opens our minds and hearts to experience the life-giving energy flowing through events and encounters.

3. The third practice is following the soul force no matter what. As its message is worked into our lives, we encounter obstacles and opposition. By entrusting our lives to the soul force, we are given what we need at the time and realize we are living in a new country blessed by the graces only the Divine can give.

The real challenge for most of us is turning. We are so focused on controlling our material circumstances that we are distracted from embracing and becoming intimate with them. It often takes a jar from the trials and tribulations of the journey to awaken us to reality staring us in the face. A divorce, a car wreck, a diagnosis of a life-threatening disease, or the death of a loved one all are losses that remind us again and again that our journey is temporary and our connection to a greater story is essential for truth and meaning.

Currently, a pandemic is creating world-wide economic, social, and political turmoil. These hard times can become a cultural "jar" inviting us to let go of the packaged answers we have been given and turn our attention to the essentials of life-giving energy that are necessary for creative survival.

Hopefully, Pilgrim's story shows us a way of waking up to the redemptive work of the soul force. The practices move us beyond someone else's experience to be on the look-out for the soul force present in our own lives. Regardless of where we are on life's journey, whatever our age, when we take time to listen to life and reflect on our experiences, we will discover a life-giving energy inviting us to follow.

This recognition of a deeper spiritual presence is rarely instantaneous. It comes as a gradual unfolding that is a lifelong adventure.

Each turn on our path reminds us that the life-light often appears clearest in the darkest hours as it draws us beyond our illusions into a deeper truth. Such holy encounters stretch our consciousness of the soul force that sustains our journey and never lets us go.

Here I Am, Lord

By Daniel L. Schutte

I, the Lord of sea and sky,
I have heard my people cry.
All who dwell in dark and sin
my hand will save.

I, who made the starts of night,
I will make their darkness bright.
Who will bear my light to them?
Whom shall I send?

> CHORUS
> Here I am, Lord. Is it I, Lord?
> I have heard you calling in the night.
> I will go, Lord, if you lead me.
> I will hold your people in my heart.

I, the Lord of snow and rain,
I have borne my people's pain.
I have wept for love of them.
They turn away.

I will break their hearts of stone,
give them hearts for love alone.
I will speak my words to them.
Whom shall I send?

CHORUS
Here I am, Lord. Is it I, Lord?
have heard you calling in the night.
I will go, Lord, if you lead me.
I will hold your people in my heart.

I, the Lord of wind and flame,
I will tend the poor and lame.
I will set a feast for them.
My hand will save.

Finest bread I will provide,
till their hearts be satisfied.
I will give my life to them.
Whom shall I send?

CHORUS
Here I am, Lord. Is it I, Lord?
I have heard you calling in the night.
I will go, Lord, if you lead me.
I will hold your people in my heart.

About the Author

Lloyd Griffith is a graduate of Duke University and Duke Divinity School. He received a master's degree in counseling psychology from Lesley University and a Certificate in Spiritual Formation from Columbia Theological Seminary. He is involved with experiential learning in small groups through a career in resident camping, centering prayer, retreats, and pilgrimages. He can be reached at lloydgriffith31@gmail.com.